OMNIVM LVX CIVIVM

BOSTON
PUBLIC
LIBRARY

THE THING IN THE SWAMP
And More Not-So-Scary Stories

THE THING IN THE SWAMP

And More Not-So-Scary Stories

by William E. Warren

illustrated by Edward Frascino

Prentice-Hall, Inc.
Englewood Cliffs, New Jersey

Printed in the United States of America   ·J

Prentice-Hall International, Inc., London
Prentice-Hall of Australia, Pty. Ltd., Sydney
Prentice-Hall Canada, Inc., Toronto
Prentice-Hall of India Private Ltd., New Delhi
Prentice-Hall of Japan, Inc., Tokyo
Prentice-Hall of Southeast Asia Pte. Ltd., Singapore
Whitehall Books Limited, Wellington, New Zealand
Editora Prentice-Hall do Brasil LTDA., Rio de Janeiro

10 9 8 7 6 5 4 3 2 1

Library of Congress Cataloging in Publication Data

Warren, William E.
    The thing in the swamp and more not-so-scary stories.

    Summary: A collection of tales of seemingly frightening
and horrible situations, each resolved in a harmless,
ordinary outcome or explanation.
    1. Horror tales, American.   2. Children's stories,
American.   [1. Horror stories.   2. Humorous stories.
3. Short stories]   I. Frascino, Edward, ill.   II. Title.
PZ7.W2572Th   1984   [Fic.]   84-6769
ISBN 0-13-917196-7

For
those who remain,
Margaret, Bigma, and George;
and for
those who are missed,
Millie, Betty, and Joe

WARNING!!!

The four stories contained in this book do not progress in normal order. For reasons that will become obvious as you read, each story has been divided into sections. These sections are separated from each other by sections from other stories.

Do not read the book straight through from cover to cover. Instead, follow the directions at the end of each section of the story you're reading.

To begin, turn to the next page and select the story you want to read.

CONTENTS

THE THING IN THE SWAMP

"This is really dumb!" Lisa complains, shielding her eyes from the sun's glare. "I don't know why I ever agreed to go fishing with you two, anyway."

"I don't know what you're complaining about," Terry replies as he watches his cork lying motionless in the still water. "We're the ones who are doing all the work. If you don't like to fish, Lisa, just sit back and enjoy the sun."

"I'd rather be back home enjoying the soap operas," Lisa growls.

You and your friends Terry and Lisa are sitting in an aluminum jonboat, fishing along the edge of a small lake hidden deep within a primitive swamp. Water lilies dot the surface along the shoreline. Overhead, a hawk circles lazily among the air currents, searching for small animals scurrying in the underbrush.

1

"This is the life," Terry says with a smile, ignoring Lisa's earlier comments. "Fishing, friends, cold drinks—"

"And mosquitos, sunburn, and boredom," Lisa finishes.

Terry glances sharply at Lisa. "You know, Lisa, you could be replaced by almost anything."

"Why?" Lisa replies angrily. "Because I hate squishy old worms?"

"No," Terry laughs, "because *you're* a squishy old worm!"

Suddenly, a movement by the shoreline catches your eye. It's an alligator, a large one, nine or ten feet long. The alligator is gliding smoothly through a patch of lily pads.

Excited as you are at seeing the 'gator, you manage to keep quiet. If Lisa sees it, there's no telling what she'll do.

You glance quickly at Terry and Lisa. They haven't seen the alligator yet. Terry is reeling in his line.

"No fish there," Terry says, eyeing the dark water disgustedly. "Think I'll try the other side of the boat for awhile. Maybe over by that log floating in the water."

Before you can stop him, Terry flips the line, float, and hook toward the 'gator. The float hits the water with a soft *plop*!

"No, Terry!" you cry, but it's too late. The alligator snaps viciously, and the hook and float disappear between its enormous jaws.

"Hot dog. I'm gonna catch me a 'gator!" Terry tugs furiously at the line as Lisa shrieks in horror.

"Terry, wait!" you hiss. Terry isn't listening, though; he's too busy trying to pull the alligator toward the boat.

You grab Terry's arm. He turns his head to listen to you, but continues to tug at his line.

"Listen, Terry," you say frantically. "What are you gonna do if you reel in the 'gator all the way to the boat? What then?"

Terry smiles sickly. "I hadn't thought of that."

Suddenly, the alligator lurches sideways, tilting the boat. The sudden movement catches Lisa off balance and tips her into the murky water.

Then, without warning, the alligator sinks beneath the surface. Terry's fishing line goes slack.

You know all too well what that means. The 'gator is heading toward the boat.

And toward Lisa.

(Turn to page 18)

THE MUMMY'S CURSE

"Dr. Bayless," you call. "Over here! I think I've found something!"

Lisa's father hurries over to inspect your find. He studies it carefully from several different angles as a large crowd of Egyptian laborers gathers around the two of you. "I think we're on the right track—yes, here it is: the inscription. You've done it; you've found the Lost Tomb of Anankha!*"

Your mind has already carried you thousands of miles away from Egypt and the Valley of the Kings. You're at a press conference, answering the questions of reporters eager to discuss your find. Behind you, the President of the United States and other dignitaries stand waiting to congratulate you.

Your discovery, the Lost Tomb of Anankha, has been described as "the greatest archaeological find since King Tut."

---

*pronounced Uh-non'-ka.

5

Your picture has been on the cover of *Time, Newsweek, Life,* and practically every other major magazine and newspaper in the world. Johnny Carson can't wait to have you on *The Tonight Show.*

A reporter is asking you a question when suddenly a dark, bearded man bursts through the crowd and strides toward you. He is carrying a gun in his hand.

"Infidel! Unbeliever!" he shouts, aiming the gun directly at your head. "You were warned. The inscription—the curse of Anankha! You disregarded it, and now you must pay with your life! Death to unbelievers!"

He squeezes the trigger. Your ears ring with the deafening explosion

(Turn to page 12)

THE GREAT WHITE SHARK

You're gliding effortlessly through crystal-clear blue ocean water, propelling yourself along with easy kicks of your swim fins. Every time you breathe, clouds of silvery bubbles float to the surface thirty-five feet above you.

A few feet away, your friend Lisa Bayless is moving easily beneath the scuba tank strapped to her back. The two of you are swimming in the shallow Gulf Stream waters of the Bahamas.

You're looking for sharks.

You've seen sharks before; Lisa hasn't, except in photographs—but you've convinced her that sharks aren't really dangerous.

Lisa doesn't really believe you, of course. She never believes anything you say. Still, you've managed to convince her that she won't be in any danger as long as she doesn't upset any sharks she meets.

You're glad that Lisa hasn't asked you how to avoid upsetting a shark. You don't have an answer for that question. No one else does, either, except for telling you to stay out of the water. Sharks are dangerous, unpredictable creatures—sort of like your little brother Mitchie when he's in a biting mood.

You're swimming along the edge of a coral reef. To your right, a sharp drop-off of darker blue water marks the beginning of the deeper ocean.

Below you, thousands of fish of every imaginable size, shape, and color swim unconcernedly, never straying more than a dozen feet from the safety of the reef. They don't seem to notice you and Lisa swimming above them.

Suddenly, a huge, dark shape slides past you along the edge of the reef. It's so large that at first you think it must be a whale. As the fish glides past, though, your stomach knots into a cold lump of fear.

One glance at the dorsal fin convinces you that the fish is a shark.

A fifty-foot shark.

Lisa has seen it, too. She tugs at your shoulder and motions violently toward shore.

You nod, scarcely daring to breathe. But before you can swim away, the great shark turns. With smooth strokes of its tail fin, it propels itself directly toward you.

The shark's mouth is open slightly, permitting water to flow through its gills. Its jaws are large enough to swallow the two of you in one bite.

You and Lisa watch in quiet terror as the fish swims toward you. It glides silently past, cutting you off from shore. Then, having inspected you and sensed your helplessness, the shark turns and lunges toward you and your friend Lisa.

(Turn to page 34)

GRIZZLY!

The pain in your broken leg is unbelievable. Still, you're lucky to be alive. The fall from the mountaintop should have killed you.

You're sitting on a narrow ledge with your back against the cold mountainside. Your feet and lower legs are dangling out into space. A thousand feet below you, a choppy river crawls through a steep canyon carved out of the rock by nature over millions of years.

Beyond you, tall and stately mountains stretch into the distance as far as you can see. It's early summer now, and some of the taller peaks still bear their snowy caps.

It is a beautiful sight. At any other time, you'd be enjoying the view. Instead, you find yourself shivering, partly from the morning chill in the air. And partly from fear.

Fear, because you're still shaken after your fall from the mountaintop fifteen feet above you. Fear, because your position on the narrow ledge you're sitting on is anything but secure. Loose rocks fall away into space every time you move.

And fear, because you're not alone.

You've heard the sounds. The deep, rumbling noises nearby, like a sports car idling low. You know what the sounds are, too. The realization comes like a dive into a cold mountain stream, sending sudden shock waves through you.

It's a mountain lion.

A cougar. A puma. Call it what you will, it's the most dangerous killer of the mountains.

Somewhere nearby, a mountain lion is stalking you.

(Turn to page 16)

of applause and cheering from the large group of Egyptian workers standing nearby. They are as excited as you are about your discovery. It could turn out to be one of the greatest finds in the history of Egyptian tombs.

Meanwhile, Dr. Bayless is talking to you, trying to make himself heard above the cheering. He is explaining the inscription over the concealed doorway.

"It's a warning," he says loudly. "A curse, actually. But we're not going to believe any such nonsense as a curse made five thousand years ago, are we?"

You answer his question with a question of your own. "What does the inscription say, Dr. Bayless?"

The professor leans forward and reads, "Painful and violent death will be the reward of whoever enters this chamber and disturbs the slumber of Anankha."

Painful and violent death?

You try to gulp down the sudden knot of fear that is forming in your throat. Beads of perspiration pop out on your forehead.

You know that if somebody touched you, you'd scream.

Dr. Bayless reads on and then turns back to you. "Apparently, Anankha was in his early teens when he became Pharaoh. He was considered a god by his subjects, until one of them slid a carving knife between his shoulder blades. They didn't have time to build a pyramid to bury him in, so they slipped him into a tomb that was being prepared for a well-to-do citizen. That's why no one has discovered Anankha's remains before now."

You glance at the concealed tomb. It's located just below the rim of a small gully. The entrance is hidden by several large rocks; the largest one fits snugly against the doorway. The inscription can be seen only by lying on top of the large boulder in front of the doorway.

"I wouldn't have found the tomb either," you say, "if I hadn't stumbled and fallen onto the boulder. They really did a good job of hiding it."

"Yes, they did," Dr. Bayless says. "But you must remember, the Egyptians were not cavemen. They had a highly developed civilization for their time. They studied astronomy and mathematics. With their primitive tools they created monuments such as the Pyramids that have lasted for fifty centuries or more. They preserved their dead with such skill that mummies have been found with their skin still intact."

And, you think glumly, *they made death curses against those who disturbed their dead.*

"Well!" Dr. Bayless says, climbing down from the boulder and brushing himself off. "Let's see what the tomb looks like inside, shall we?"

He gives orders to the workers in Egyptian, and several of them scurry off. Soon they're back with arms full of equipment for prying the boulder away from the doorway.

Ninety minutes later they're finished. Overhead, the sun beats down relentlessly, bathing the faces of workers and watchers alike with perspiration.

Dr. Bayless hands you a large flashlight identical to the one he is carrying. He motions for you to precede him into the tomb.

"Go ahead," he says when you hesitate. "It's your discovery; you should have the honor of being the first to enter. No one has been in there since Anankha was buried."

Yes, you think, *and no one has come out alive since then, either!*

Taking a deep breath, you step into the chamber and proceed cautiously down a long, dark stairway carved out of the ground. Dr. Bayless follows you.

As you walk slowly down the stairs, you hear Dr. Bayless speaking softly, almost reverently. His words float in the darkness and touch your ears like the soft breath of something almost, but not quite, dead for scores of centuries: "Anankha's wife will have been buried with him."

"Did they kill her, too?" you ask in a trembling voice. You're afraid that you already know what the professor's answer will be.

"No," he replies, "they would have buried her alive with her husband. She was supposed to protect and guide his soul on its journey to its final resting place."

They buried her alive! You reel in horror at the idea. And then something worse crosses your mind—maybe she isn't dead yet! Maybe she's waiting for you somewhere ahead in the darkness, with her bony fingers curled around a long, curved dagger.

No sooner does the grisly thought enter your mind than you *see* the dagger gleaming in your flashlight's glow, drawing closer and closer to you. And then, to your everlasting horror, you see the woman, Anankha's bride, watching you with eyes that have not seen daylight in five thousand years.

"You're supposed to be dead!" you shout. Your words echo hollowly in the narrow passageway. But she's *not* dead, you realize. She's three feet away, reaching for you with one hand. In her other hand, a razor-sharp dagger is drawn back, ready to strike.

(Turn to page 19)

Suddenly, you hear it again, only louder—closer—this time. Ever so slowly, you try to stand up, but the pain is too great. Every time you move, a sharp pain stabs through your leg like a dentist's drill hitting a nerve.

Then, without warning, the lion steps into view, twenty feet to your right on the ledge. It's larger than you expected it to be. And meaner looking, too.

You stare in silent horror at the big cat, and press back even harder against the rock wall behind you.

The cougar watches you coldly, intently. Its lower jaw hangs open to reveal a set of sharp fangs that could grind you into hamburger meat.

You glance around quickly, searching for something—any-thing!—to help you escape or defend yourself.

Even if you had two good legs, though, there's nowhere to go. The ledge you're sitting on extends only a few feet to your left before it fades into the mountainside.

A thousand feet below you, the shallow, rocky river roars and tumbles along as it has done for thousands of years.

You're trapped, with nowhere to run to, nowhere to hide. There's nothing you can do to protect yourself from the great beast that is slowly, cautiously moving toward you along the slender ledge.

The cougar seems to sense your fear and helplessness. It pauses ten feet away and snarls menacingly. Its upper lip curls back to reveal the large canine teeth that it uses to tear meat away from the bones of its victims.

You want to scream, but all that comes out of your throat is a sick, whimpering noise. Your eyes bulge in terror as you realize that Death is standing less than four yards away from you.

(Turn to page 24)

You struggle to keep the narrow aluminum boat from over-turning and dumping you and Terry into the water with Lisa. "We've got to get her out of the water, Terry!" you shout as Lisa splashes her way to the surface. "The 'gator's after her!"

The two of you quickly haul Lisa into the boat. Drenched from head to toe, sputtering and crying, she's trembling despite the afternoon heat.

Fear can do that to you.

Suddenly, you hear a loud *thump* and feel the boat jarred wildly from side to side as something passes beneath it. Lisa screams.

"Watch out!" you hear yourself shouting. "The alligator is attacking the boat!"

(Turn to page 22)

"The Egyptians were excellent artists," Dr. Bayless says, admiring the painting on the wall. "The woman holding the dagger is Anankha's bride. She must have been quite a beautiful young woman. And I was right, too: she is guarding the soul of her departed husband. When we reach the burial chamber, we'll find her waiting for us."

Yeah, you think, *I just bet we will!*

Finally, you reach the bottom of the stairs. Your flashlight's slender beam shows that the corridor makes a sharp left turn fifteen feet ahead.

When you turn the corner, your heart leaps in sudden fear. You expect to find the hideous, undead faces of Anankha and his young bride staring at you in the cold light of your flashlight's beam, and icy fingers reaching for you from somewhere beyond the grave.

Nothing's there, though. Ahead, you can see that the corridor continues for maybe fifty feet before it ends in a blank stone wall.

"That would be the burial chamber," Dr. Bayless says. "It's not a wall, but a stone door that was slid into place after the pharaoh was placed in his burial vault."

"How will we get into it?" Your voice sounds hollow and lifeless in the musty air.

"The same way we got into the tomb," Dr. Bayless says. He tells you to go back and have some of the men bring tools to pry the door open. Relief floods over you; you were afraid he was going to suggest that you stay down there alone while he returned to the surface to get some men and equipment.

"On second thought, maybe I'd better go instead," the professor says. "You don't speak Egyptian, and you don't know which tools to bring."

"Maybe we'd both better go," you suggest weakly.

Dr. Bayless laughs. "Nonsense. You'll be perfectly safe. Nothing has been alive in here for thousands of years."

The professor turns and retreats down the corridor before you can tell him that it's nothing alive that scares you.

It's the dead things. Or maybe the not-quite-dead things.

The ancient Egyptians were great at preserving the bodies of their dead; we know that. But suppose—just suppose—that they were also experts at preserving the bodies of people who weren't dead.

Or that maybe they had ways of bringing the dead back to life . . .

Dr. Bayless turns the corner, and soon even the sounds of his footsteps receding into the distance are gone.

You're alone. All alone.

You know how the bride of Anankha must have felt when they rolled the stone door into place, sealing her in the tomb with her beloved.

And when her candles were used up, she faced the prospect of spending the next five thousand years in the blackest darkness imaginable.

The only sounds in the lonely corridor are your heavy, frightened breathing and the relentless hammering of your heart. Those sounds, and the light tapping of footsteps moving quietly toward you along the corridor.

"Dr. Bayless, is that you?" Pinpricks of fear dance up and down your spine.

You listen in vain for an answer, but all you can hear is the soft whisper of footsteps creeping ever nearer.

There's good news and bad news about the mysterious footsteps, you realize:

The good news is that they're approaching you from the entrance to the tomb, not from the burial chamber.

The bad news is that your escape route is cut off. You're at the mercy of whoever is approaching you.

"Dr. Bayless?" you call out, inching forward. Suddenly, you find yourself struggling against the icy grip of

(Turn to page 28)

Terry leans over and peers into the water beneath the boat. "No, it's not the 'gator. We just went over a log."

You glance at Lisa. "Are you all right?"

She nods. "I'll be okay. Just get me back to camp."

"There goes the alligator," Terry says casually, pointing to his right. You turn in time to see the big 'gator gliding silently into a patch of lily pads near the opposite shoreline. Its powerful tail creates ripples in the water behind it like a series of capital *S*'s.

"Hey, that was neat!" Terry says, beaming. He's the kind of guy who would ride an avalanche down a mountain for kicks.

"Weren't you scared, Terry?" Lisa asks as you and Terry begin paddling again. "I know *I* was."

"Nothing scares me," Terry says. "I don't know the meaning of the word *fear.*"

"I don't doubt that," you reply drily. "You haven't passed a reading or spelling test in the last four months!"

"I get As in Band, though," Terry protests. "Mr. Symonds, the band director, calls me the 'flower of the musical world: a budding genius.' "

Lisa snorts. "What he means is that you're a blooming idiot!"

The afternoon sun is beginning to dip below the treeline when the three of you finally reach the campsite. Terry's Uncle Ned is working over a small campfire, preparing supper. He smiles and waves as you approach.

Uncle Ned—he insists that all three of you call him that— is a large, happy man. He's a biologist at a big university. His specialty is the study of reptiles, and he loves his work. He takes his pet, a five-foot indigo snake, along with him when he travels.

Uncle Ned invited the three of you along for a weekend trip into the swamp. Lisa didn't want to go, but Terry convinced her that it would be fun. She probably wishes now that she hadn't come.

As for you, well . . . you'd do practically anything to get away from your little brother Mitchie for a day or two.

Sitting in front of the campfire, the three of you tell Uncle Ned about your adventure with the alligator. He's concerned, but not worried.

"It's not smart to play around with the alligators, Terry," Uncle Ned says, frowning at his nephew. "Alligators don't eat humans, but they're dangerous anyway. If that had been a mother with babies, she might have attacked you."

Terry promises never to do anything foolish like that again.

"I hope not," Uncle Ned says. "It took a lot of convincing to talk your parents into letting you come along with me for the weekend. If they knew you were taking chances like that, they'd never let you go anywhere with me again."

Suddenly, you feel something brushing lightly against your leg. You glance down to find a large, dark-colored snake winding slowly around your feet.

Your jaws drop open. Sudden terror races through you like a wildfire out of control.

You want to scream, but no sounds come from your open mouth. It's as if your whole body is made of stone. All you can do is stare helplessly at the ugly reptile at your feet.

(Turn to page 27)

Strangely, you find yourself wondering why you ever decided to go hiking alone in the mountains in the first place. Dad warned you last night not to. He said you'd get in trouble, or maybe get hurt, if you went off on your own without an adult along.

But who listens to adults? They're always telling you things like that, trying to scare you out of having a good time.

Only this time Dad was right.

You climbed out of your sleeping bag while everyone else was still asleep, dressed quietly, and tiptoed away from the others in the early morning light.

You wanted to find excitement and high adventure.

You found it, too.

You walked for miles before you reached the mountaintop. While you were enjoying the view, you must have moved too close to the edge. Your foot slipped in the wet grass and down you went, over the side of the mountain and onto the narrow ledge fifteen feet below.

Landing on the ledge saved your life—but it also broke your leg and left you helpless.

And now . . . you can almost feel the hot breath of the huge mountain lion as it snarls its hatred for you. You pick up small rocks and throw them at the cougar, but it does no good. You might as well be trying to stop a rhino with a BB-gun.

Suddenly, a large, hairy creature lumbers onto the ledge behind the cougar. One glance tells you that the huge, grayish-brown beast is a grizzly bear. The grizzly growls a warning which is quickly answered by the puma's shrill scream.

The grizzly rises to an upright position, pawing the air angrily. Confused, the mountain lion snarls fiercely, takes a single step backward toward you, and then leaps toward the grizzly.

Howling in rage, the grizzly swings his giant paw and swats the cougar off the ledge as easily as a human might brush a gnat away from his face. The cougar cartwheels through a thousand feet of space before it lands on the rockpile at the base of the cliff. It does not move.

Your first reaction is one of relief at having escaped the cougar. Your relief is short-lived, though; one glance at the grizzly reminds you that an even greater danger faces you.

You might have had a chance against the cougar; after all, it outweighed you by only about fifty pounds. But the grizzly bear weighs at least six hundred pounds.

And judging by the way it is shuffling slowly, angrily toward you, it is obvious that the grizzly has no intention of sharing the ledge with you or anyone else.

(Turn to page 29)

"Herky, stop that!" Uncle Ned says to his pet indigo snake. He reaches down and gently picks up the snake, cradling it in his arms.

"You're a bad boy, Herky, scaring our friends like that." Uncle Ned rubs the snake gently.

"It's okay," you say, still weak-kneed with fright. "He wasn't bothering me." It's not true, though. Your idea of a fun weekend definitely does *not* include snakes—even pet snakes —using you for a playground.

"Why do you call him Herky?" you ask as Lisa rises. Her wet clothes are sticking to her; you guess that she's going to her tent to change.

Uncle Ned smiles. "Herky is short for Herky-Jerky, because that's the way he crawls."

Near her tent, Lisa pauses. "Oh, look at the pretty little snake! It's red and yellow and black, and . . ." She leans over to pick it up.

"No, Lisa!" you shout as her hand nears the snake at her feet. "That's a coral snake! They're poisonous!"

Your warning is too late. Lisa has already picked up the snake. The smile on her face freezes into a look of horror as your words finally sink in.

"Get rid of it, Lisa!" you manage to say around the lump of fear forming in your throat.

She does nothing, though, except stare at the deadly eighteen-inch snake she is holding in her hands. Its poison is as deadly as a king cobra's venom.

(Turn to page 32)

the most powerful panic you've ever known. You feel an uncontrollable urge to run, even if it means stumbling into the deadly embrace of the mummy or his bride.

You sprint down the dark passageway, turn the corner . . . and halt suddenly, gasping in speechless, mind-numbing terror at the sight before you.

There, bathed in the dim light of your flashlight's glow, is the young girl you dreaded seeing.

At that worst of all possible moments, your flashlight beam flickers once, twice, and then goes out.

Footsteps pad softly toward you in the darkness.

Unable to move, or even to speak, you shut your eyes in terror. Then you gasp as a cold hand drops onto your shoulder. Slender, icy fingers clamp down in a death-grip on your collarbone. You open your eyes to see the face of

(Turn to page 30)

The grizzly moves toward you slowly, studying you. Maybe it won't hurt me if I don't upset it, you decide, gritting your teeth and trying to remain calm.

It doesn't work, though; the grizzly growls a warning as it moves to within three feet of you. You can feel the bear's hot breath on your face. You know that it's going to kill you.

But then, as the enraged grizzly roars and swings a huge paw toward your face, the world goes black before your eyes. You slide backward, and feel the rough mountainside scraping against your back as you slump over onto your side.

Dimly, you feel something hitting your face, hard, but somehow it doesn't hurt. You open your eyes to find the grizzly shaking you violently, its two-inch claws gouging into your shoulders.

"Please don't kill me!" you shout helplessly.

(Turn to page 36)

Lisa Bayless, the professor's daughter and one of your best friends. Lisa's flashlight suddenly comes on, throwing a strong, healthy glow.

"I'm glad you're here, Lisa," you say weakly. "I was beginning to think that you were a mummy."

"Don't be silly," Lisa replies. "I'm not even married. I heard you yelling. I figured that you had gotten scared. What's the matter with your flashlight?"

"I don't know. It doesn't work. The batteries must be dead."

"Maybe it's just a loose connection," Lisa suggests. "Try hitting it with the heel of your hand. Mine wasn't working a few minutes ago."

You follow her advice, and to your surprise the light returns, as strong as ever.

"Where's your father?" you ask.

"He's getting everything ready. He'll be along shortly. He told me to go on ahead. You really were scared, weren't you?"

"I suppose you wouldn't have been afraid of being down here by yourself."

"Of course not," Lisa replies. "I've been in tombs like this before."

"Alone?"

"Well . . . yes." You know Lisa isn't telling the truth. She has always been afraid of the dark.

But if that's true—and it is—then why was she willing to come down here by herself?

"Where is the burial chamber?" Lisa asks. You lead her around the corner. After the two of you have gone maybe ten feet down the passageway, Lisa's flashlight flickers off.

"Darn!" she says, pounding at the flashlight, "it's not working. Give me yours for a minute."

You hand her your flashlight. She walks a few feet away from you toward the burial chamber, working on her own flashlight.

"Can you fix it?" you ask, watching Lisa.

"I think so." Then, as she casually glances up at you, Lisa's face twists into a hideous scowl. Her scream is a high-pitched shriek that pierces the darkness like a knife.

"What's the matter?" you shout. But before Lisa can answer, two things happen at once.

The flashlight in Lisa's hand—your flashlight—flickers off again, plunging the passageway into total darkness.

And powerful hands—not Lisa's—wrap themselves tightly around your throat, squeezing tighter and tighter until your tongue hangs out and you feel yourself slipping into unconsciousness.

(Turn to page 38)

"Don't move, Lisa," Uncle Ned warns. He walks quickly over to her and takes the snake out of her hands. Lisa, shaking all over, breathes a huge sigh of relief.

"It's not a coral snake," Uncle Ned says, admiring the colorful little snake. "It's a scarlet king snake. They're harmless."

"It could have fooled me," Lisa says in a trembling voice.

"That's right, Lisa," Uncle Ned says. "It *did* fool you. And that's why you have to be careful in the swamp. I knew it wasn't a coral snake as soon as I saw it. But I was afraid it might bite you if you moved too quickly."

"But if the snake isn't poisonous, what difference does it make whether it bites you?" Terry asks.

"Even nonpoisonous snakebites hurt," Uncle Ned answers patiently. "It may not poison you, but it still hurts."

"How did you know it wasn't a coral snake?" you ask. "I thought coral snakes were red and yellow and black."

"They are," Uncle Ned replies, "but other snakes like this scarlet king snake have those colors, too. The difference is in the way the colors are arranged. On the coral snake, every red band is touching a yellow band. The harmless snakes' red bands are next to black bands.

"Another way of putting it is

Red touch black, good for Jack.
Red touch yellow, kill a fellow.

Think you can remember that, Lisa?"

She nods.

"Or you can always look at the snake's nose. If it's red or brown, it's a harmless snake. Coral snakes have black noses."

"I thought snakes didn't have noses," Terry says.

Uncle Ned shakes his head slowly and smiles. He's used to Terry. "You're right, Terry. Snakes don't have noses. So all you have to do is look where the nose would be if it had one."

"Why are some snakes colored to look like other snakes?" Lisa asks.

"It's part of nature's way of defending helpless animals," Uncle Ned replies. "Other animals will see those colors, too, and they'll be fooled just as you were, Lisa. They'll think the snake is a coral snake, and they'll leave it alone."

"Hey, that's neat!" Terry says. Terry thinks everything is neat.

"Yes, it *is* neat, Terry," Uncle Ned says. "But if you think *that's* neat, wait until after supper when I tell you the story of the Thing in the Swamp."

"Oh, boy!" Terry says, grinning broadly. "I love ghost stories!"

"You *are* a ghost story," Lisa says, frowning.

A shadow of concern crosses Uncle Ned's face as he watches his nephew across the campfire. "It isn't a ghost story, Terry. It's real." He glances around uneasily. "Something's out there. Something big. And evil. It probably knows we're here, too."

Lisa shudders. Hugging herself, she moves closer to the fire for protection.

"Hey, it doesn't scare me!" Terry announces bravely.

"I'm sure it doesn't," Lisa agrees, "but if you don't back up a few feet, Terry, your pants are going to catch fire!"

(Turn to page 40)

The shark is as large as a locomotive.

Luckily for you, it's a whale shark.

They're harmless, the whale sharks. Rare and gentle giants of the ocean, they feed on extremely tiny animals called plankton.

Not humans.

The whale shark slides past the two of you on its way to wherever whale sharks go.

Lisa glances at you. Her eyes are wide with fear behind her swim mask. You want to tell her to relax, take it easy. But you can't say anything with the breathing tube in your mouth.

It doesn't matter, though. She wouldn't believe you, anyway.

You and Lisa are swimming at an angle slightly away from the drop-off. You notice that Lisa has lagged behind slightly.

Without stopping to wait for her, you turn to see what's the matter.

Lisa has the same wild-eyed look of terror on her face as before. At first, you think she's still frightened from seeing the whale shark. But no, she's waving her arms wildly and pointing beyond you.

She's trying to warn you.

But warn you of what?

You turn back . . . and find yourself swimming directly into the gaping mouth of a gigantic

(Turn to page 43)

But it's not a grizzly bear that is shaking you. It's your little brother Mitchie.

"What—what happened?" you ask groggily, still half asleep.

"You had a nightmare and fell out of bed," Mitchie replies. "C'mon, get up! You promised to take me for a hike in the mountains today!"

"No, I didn't," you protest sleepily, staggering to your feet. Beyond you, sunlight is streaming in through one of the two windows in the room.

"Yeah, you did. You said last night that we could hike through the woods to Bald Rock Mountain this morning."

Why, you wonder, do you agree to things like that? Your little brother Mitchie is only six years old, but he's *such* a pain.

"Get dressed, we gotta go," Mitchie says loudly. He's already dressed. But since he's only six years old, his shirt is on backwards, his socks don't match, his shoes are on the wrong feet, and his laces aren't tied.

"Okay, okay," you hiss, "but keep quiet! If we wake Mom and Dad, they'll be mad. What time is it, anyway?"

"How do I know?" Mitchie replies in a half-whisper. "You're the one who can tell time."

Ten minutes later, you're standing outside the cabin your family has rented for the week. Its green walls and green roof remind you of a giant potted plant. The cabin is nestled in a wide valley between mountain ranges. One end of the valley is open, with woods extending as far as the eye can see.

At the other end of the valley, Bald Rock Mountain towers above the other mountains like a giant among dwarves.

"C'mon, slowpoke, let's go!" Mitchie says impatiently.

"Why don't you go on ahead, Mitchie?" you ask, yawning loudly. You wish he *would* go on ahead, too, so you could go back to sleep for a few more hours.

"But there are *bears* in the woods," Mitchie says. "And I

might get lost if I go by myself. You don't want me to be eaten by a bear or get lost, do you?"

You smile at the idea. "No, I guess not. Mom would just make me go find you. Let's go."

"How far is it to the mountain?" Mitchie asks as the two of you pad softly through the dark, deep forest. Around you, the tall evergreen trees reach heavenward like thick green spikes.

"It's about twenty feet closer than it was the last time you asked," you grumble. You've been walking for twenty minutes, but Bald Rock seems no closer than when you left the cabin.

"We're not getting any closer to it," Mitchie says, as if reading your mind.

"Sure we are." You learned a long time ago not to agree with Mitchie. He's hard enough to live with already. "The mountain just *looks* like it's a long way off."

Twenty minutes later, the mountain still looks no closer. Distances can be deceiving in the mountains, you decide.

Hiking in the mountains isn't as easy as you'd thought it would be, either. For one thing, it's tiring. For another, it's almost impossible to walk in a straight line. There are large boulders and thick bushes of mountain laurel to walk around, trees to avoid, ditches to cross. Finally, there's the ever-present danger of stepping on one of the poisonous snakes in the area.

"I'm thirsty," Mitchie complains.

"Two minutes ago you were hungry," you reply, looking back at Mitchie as you step over a rotten log. "And five minutes before that you—"

Suddenly, the quiet stillness around you is shattered by a sharp, rattling noise at your feet. You look down at your feet in horror, realizing that you've just stepped on a rattl-

(Turn to page 47)

Lisa thumbs the ON button of the flashlight in her hand, and light returns to the passageway. "Terry, stop it! Enough is enough!"

"Huh? Oh, okay," Terry Willis says, releasing you. You sag to the floor, rubbing your neck.

"Sorry," Terry says. "Guess I don't know my own strength." Terry weighs much more than you do, and most of it is muscle.

"Where have you been?" Lisa asks Terry.

"Getting my beauty sleep."

"You're about five thousand years behind," you grumble, glaring at Terry and climbing to your feet.

Terry ignores you. "Hey, this is neat! Pop would *love* to be here."

Terry's father is a mortician, and Terry loves to joke about it. "Yep," he goes on. "Pop would think he was one lucky stiff." You and Lisa groan.

"Here we go again," Lisa says.

"That's right," Terry continues. "You kill 'em, we chill 'em. Remember our motto: *We keep the 'fun' in funeral.* "

Sounds at the other end of the corridor announce the return of Dr. Bayless and his assistants. Lisa gives you your flashlight and thumbs hers on. Now you know why she was willing to come down here alone when she's afraid of the dark; she wasn't alone. Terry was with her. They planned the whole thing beforehand!

Dr. Bayless and the workmen arrive and begin working on the door. Twenty minutes later, they have wedged it open far enough for the four of you—Professor Bayless, you, Lisa, and Terry—to squeeze through.

Dr. Bayless motions for you to enter the burial chamber.

You glance at Lisa and Terry. They're both grinning, expecting you to chicken out. Well, there's no way you're going to give them that satisfaction!

You inhale deeply once and step through the doorway. Immediately, before anyone else can pass through the narrow opening, you hear the harsh, grating sound of the stone door sliding shut behind you, sealing you off from your friends and imprisoning you in the burial chamber with Anankha and his bride!

A surge of mind-chilling terror jolts through you like an electric shock. You whirl around, open-mouthed, to find

(Turn to page 52)

"Tell us about the Thing in the Swamp, Uncle Ned!" Terry urges for at least the fiftieth time since the four of you finished supper.

"I guess it's late enough now to get started with the story," Uncle Ned says, eyeing the graying sky and shadows turning into darkness. You, Terry, and Lisa are sitting around the campfire, watching as Uncle Ned stokes the embers and tosses a couple of branches onto the small, crackling blaze.

Beyond the range of firelight, the night is alive with strange sounds. An owl hooting. A loon calling. The grunting of 'gators in the distance. A chorus of frogs, toads, and crickets nearby.

And Uncle Ned's voice, speaking as quietly as slow death.

"The first to disappear was Skeeter Vincent's dog," Uncle Ned says. "Then, when Skeeter came back here to find his dog, *he* vanished, too. Just like that."

"What happened to them?" Terry asks.

"Nobody knows. Some folks say they wandered into quick-sand, but it's not likely. Skeeter lived around this swamp all his life. He could cross it on stilts, blind-folded and walking backward, without stepping in quicksand. More likely, Skeeter and his dog met up with the Thing in the Swamp."

"The Thing in the Swamp?" Lisa says with a shudder.

"You sound like an echo," you tell her sarcastically. "Let him tell the story, Lisa." She frowns at you, but keeps quiet as Uncle Ned continues.

"A hundred years ago, the Indians who lived here had legends about a huge monster that inhabited the swamp. Some said it was a bear, others said it was some kind of ape-like creature. Nobody knew for sure, though. All they could agree on was that it was huge, and that it walked upright like a man."

"Why couldn't they agree about what it looked like?" you ask, staring intently at Uncle Ned. You're afraid that if you take your eyes off him and glance into the darkness beyond the fire's glow, you'll see the fiery eyes of a huge beast with fangs dripping blood. And then you'll hear the grunt of rage as it charges, trampling the fire and knocking Uncle Ned aside in its eagerness to taste your flesh.

"Nobody who has seen the Thing has ever lived to tell about it," Uncle Ned replies.

"How do *you* know what it looks like?" Terry asks.

"I don't. But there were footprints—I've seen some of them myself, not too far from here—and there were rumors. You know how people love to talk about things like that." Uncle Ned smiles. In the firelight's eerie, flickering glow, he looks like a vampire.

"Judging by the size of the footprints, the Thing must be nearly seven feet tall and must weight about three hundred pounds," Uncle Ned says.

"You're not much smaller than that," Terry says to his uncle, laughing nervously.

Uncle Ned chuckles softly, only it isn't a happy laugh. It's more like the laugh of someone who's had his evil secret discovered, but knows that you're unable to do anything about it. He rises to his feet, towering over you like a mountain of darkness.

"You're right, of course," he says, curling his fingers into huge fists. "And since you've noticed that, I'm afraid I have no choice but to kill

(Turn to page 50)

underwater cave.

You'd like to explore the cave, but you don't have a lantern with you. If you had known about the cave you'd have brought along a light.

Lisa wouldn't have gone with you, though; if there's one thing she's more afraid of than sharks, it's dark places. Lisa is afraid of the dark. She says that unearthly horrors lurk in the deep shadows and corners of dark places, waiting for a suitable victim.

Waiting for you.

From out of the cave's inky blackness, a great white shark surges past you. Cold water swirls around you as the fish sweeps past in a blur.

You can see the white underbelly that gives the great white shark its name. Above, the shark's skin is gray, and covered with tiny, sharp scales called *denticles*. One touch of those scales will leave you bleeding—and once the great white shark smells blood in the water, any hope of escape will vanish. The great white shark is the largest meat-eating animal on earth.

For a moment, before the icy grip of terror freezes your mind, you wonder if maybe the shark didn't see you. But you saw the huge black eyeball move slightly in its socket as the shark swam past.

It saw you, all right. You know it did.

You know, too, that great white sharks don't have to be upset, or even hungry, to attack. Eating is more than a need for them; it's a *habit*. They'll eat anything, anywhere, anytime.

And unless things change for the better quickly, you and Lisa are going to be the next meals on the menu.

You want to escape—but where is there to go? You could never outswim a great white shark. And even if you could, Lisa couldn't.

You glance at Lisa. She's paralyzed with fear, watching the monster shark with an expression of pure horror on her face. You know the feeling; your whole body is numb with fright, as if you had suddenly discovered that the fake monsters in a carnival sideshow aren't really fake, after all.

The great white shark circles past you; despite the fear pounding through your veins, you find yourself staring in awe at the grace and beauty of its movements.

Its size alone—twenty-four feet long and weighing as much as your family car—is enough to make you feel faint.

The great white shark curls back toward you, closer this time. Its mouth is open slightly, revealing row upon row of razor-sharp, triangular, two-inch teeth.

Teeth that could rip you to shreds in less than a second.

We've got to get out of here! you think. You motion urgently to Lisa to follow you, and the two of you begin swimming wildly toward shore.

Your thrashing movements excite the shark. A shudder seems to ripple along the entire length of its body, and it springs forward to attack you.

The last insane thought you have before the shark reaches you is, *Maybe it'll get Lisa first, and give me time to get to shore.* Even before you can feel guilty for thinking such thoughts, you realize that the great white shark isn't going after Lisa at all.

It's after you.

The great white's snout is curled upward, its jaws fully extended, revealing row upon row of teeth that look like white bandsaw blades. The shark is rushing at you with the speed of a locomotive.

You stop swimming and try to twist away from the onrushing blur, but it's too late. Dinner is served.

And you're the main course.

(Turn to page 63)

ing set of keys. Yours, of course. You must have forgotten to tell Mom last night about the hole in your pocket. You slip the keychain into another pocket of your jeans.

"I'm hungry," Mitchie announces as you resume your hike.

"I thought you were thirsty, Mitchie."

"I am, but I'm hungry, too. And tired. Why are all the hills uphill? Don't any of the hills go downhill?"

"You want to turn around and go back to the cabin?"

"Uh-uh," Mitchie replies. "Maybe we'll find a Burger Queen."

"*Out here?* Mitchie, you may not have noticed, but this isn't a shopping mall. We're in the woods. There are wild animals out here—"

You stop suddenly, listening and peering into the dark woods behind you. "*What was that?*"

"What was what?" Mitchie asks. You motion for him to be quiet.

"Nothing," you say finally. "I thought I heard a noise."

"I didn't hear anything."

You frown. "Mitchie, as noisy as you are when you're walking, you couldn't hear a herd of elephants stampeding around you. You're supposed to be quiet in the woods."

"Why?" Mitchie asks, making as much noise as ever.

Before you can answer, you hear a series of crashing noises in the woods behind you. You glance at Mitchie. He nods, wide-eyed. "I heard *that.* What was it?"

"I don't know, but I don't think we ought to wait around to find out! C'mon!"

"Hey, wait for me!" Mitchie calls out as you rush headlong through the thick forest. But you aren't worried about Mitchie or poisonous snakes or anything else except getting away from whatever is behind you.

Finally, you slow down and turn cautiously to see if the animal is still pursuing you.

In your mind's eye, you see yourself turning to face the hideous, snarling jaws of an enraged grizzly.

When you turn, though, it's not there. Neither is Mitchie.

The forest is still and quiet. Tall evergreens tower above you like spires of a great cathedral.

"Mitchie!" you call out. But there's no response except the restless beating of your heart. You wait for a minute or two, calling to Mitchie without success.

For all you know, he may have been swallowed up by the earth. Or by something even worse—a grizzly.

Dad has warned you about the grizzlies in the area. There aren't many of them around any more, he said, but the ones that are left can be very dangerous to humans. They've been known to kill people who stumbled onto them while hiking in the woods.

You begin to feel guilty for leaving your little brother behind. He *is* a pest, but he's your brother, too. And he's your responsibility. If he fell and hurt himself, he could be lying helpless somewhere behind you in the woods. Or maybe he's unconscious, or even dead.

"No!" you shout, and begin trotting back toward the point where you left Mitchie. Every now and then you pause to catch your breath and call Mitchie, but there's no answer. Your fear for Mitchie's safety grows with each passing minute.

"Mitchie, are you all right? Where are you?" you call out loudly as you halt beside a boulder you passed earlier. The huge boulder is at least twelve feet high and thirty feet around.

Somewhere on the other side of the boulder, a twig snaps loudly.

You gasp in surprise and your heart leaps into your throat. "Mitchie? Is that you?"

Nothing.

"Who's there?" you ask in a shaky voice. But there's no reply, except a gentle breeze sighing in the treetops far above you.

Another twig snaps.

"C'mon, Mitchie, quit playing games," you say, trying to control the trembling in your voice. Still there's no answer.

"Okay, you asked for it." Taking a deep breath, you rush around the boulder and halt, your eyes bulging with fear. Your heart is pounding like a string of firecrackers going off.

Nothing's there.

You heave a giant sigh of relief. It was just your imagination, that's all. *It's funny*, you think, *how your mind can play tricks on you when you're scared.*

Deep in thought, you fail to notice the hairy creature rushing at you from behind. Then, a second before it clasps its huge arms around you, its deep, throaty growl sends terror flowing through you like an electric shock.

You try to run, but it's too late. Clasped around the chest by two powerful, hairy arms, you're trapped as surely as a fly in a spider web. Slowly, the arms tighten around you like steel bands, squeezing, crushing . . . and foul-smelling breath blows against your cheek as the great beast slowly turns you around, then lifts you until the two of you are face to face.

(Turn to page 58)

some of these mosquitos. They're really swarming tonight. I'm going to get some insect repellent from my tent." He turns and pads away into the darkness as quietly as a 280-pound ghost.

"That was some kind of story," Terry says quietly.

"You don't believe it, do you?" Lisa asks. Her worried expression shows that *she* believes it's true.

"Sure," Terry says. "Uncle Ned wouldn't lie about something like that."

"It's not a lie," you reply. "It's a ghost story, that's all."

"Do you really think so?" Lisa asks hopefully.

You nod. "He's just trying to scare us."

Terry frowns. "Take a look around you. Haven't you seen the eyes in the darkness out there? Who's to say that two of those eyes don't belong to the Thing in the Swamp? Or that it's not just waiting for us to go to sleep so it can attack?"

"I wish Uncle Ned would come back. I'm scared," Lisa says.

"I still don't believe it," you say. In the distance, a high-pitched, wailing sound pierces the night, sending shivers down your spine.

Terry glances from you to Lisa. "Did you hear that? It could have been the Thing!"

"Or it could have been a bobcat," you reply in a voice that is less confident than before. There *are* a lot of scary things out there. And what if one of those things happens to be a huge half-bear, half-ape that craves human flesh?

It's possible, you have to admit. Unlikely, but possible. Heck, anything's possible. You don't need the sky falling on you to tell you that.

But then, to your everlasting horror, the sky *does* fall on you, in the form of a creature landing on top of you from out of the darkness. As Terry and Lisa scream in fright, your first thought is that it's Uncle Ned playing a trick on you.

It's not Uncle Ned, though. It's exactly what Uncle Ned warned you about earlier; it's the Thing

(Turn to page 54)

Dr. Bayless and his assistants *opening* the door, not closing it. They're widening the opening so everyone can get through.

When everyone is in the room, you glance around for the first time, fearful of what you'll see.

The burial chamber is large, perhaps thirty feet square, but it looks even larger because there are surprisingly few objects in the room.

There is, of course, the burial vault itself: a large, rectangular brick structure in the center of the room. The vault is covered by a large stone slab. Inside the vault, you realize as a sudden shiver of fear lances through you, lies the earthly remains—the mummy—of Anankha, teenage pharaoh of Egypt.

Near the vault is a throne carved out of rock. Seated on the throne—or, to be more precise, lying across the stone seat—is the skeleton of Anankha's young wife.

"I think I'm gonna be sick," Terry says. Covering his mouth with his hand, he sprints from the room, making gagging sounds.

Meanwhile, Lisa is cautiously approaching the skeleton, as if she is afraid that it might leap out of the seat and attack her at any moment.

"Dad, look!" Lisa says, pointing to the skeleton. Dangling from its neck is a beautiful gold pendant inlaid with precious stones.

"It's fabulous!" Lisa breathes.

Dr. Bayless leans forward to inspect the necklace. "Yes, it is. Extremely valuable, too. I can only guess at what we'll see inside Anankha's vault. Judging by this pendant, the vault probably will be filled with priceless treasures and jewelry."

"We'll be rich!" you exclaim, beaming at Lisa and her father.

Dr. Bayless isn't smiling, though. He leans over, picks up an object that in the dim light appears to be a dagger with a long, curving blade, and straightens.

Above his flashlight's slender shaft of light, the professor squints at you coldly through his thick-lensed glasses.

"*You* won't be rich," Dr. Bayless says quietly. "Lisa won't either. I'm afraid that *I'm* going to be the only one who gets anything out of this."

He turns to his assistant. "Get them—"

"What are you going to do? Kill us?" you blurt out, eyeing the professor in sudden fear.

A scowl creases his face, turning it into a hideous, angry mask in the semidarkness.

(Turn to page 55)

he carries with him whenever he travels: his pet snake Herky.

Then Uncle Ned is back to retrieve his snake, which had dropped out of an overhanging tree into your lap.

"Herky loves to play jokes on people," Uncle Ned says.

Some joke, you think, wondering how fried indigo snake would taste. Probably terrible.

"Tell us some more about the Thing in the Swamp!" Terry urges.

Uncle Ned yawns and stretches mightily. "It's bedtime. Besides, there's not much to tell. If you want to know what it looks like, you'll have to see it."

"But it kills everyone who sees it," Lisa protests.

Uncle Ned smiles. "Then you'd better not let it see you watching it."

"But how will—Oh, never mind!" Lisa says. Then, yawning loudly, she announces that she's going to bed. "And that snake better not crawl into my sleeping bag tonight, either," she adds, meaning Uncle Ned's pet indigo snake.

"Hey!" Terry shouts angrily. Without warning, he sends a fist whistling toward Lisa's jaw. Lisa tries to duck away, but she's too late. She howls in fear as Terry's hand makes contact with her unprotected jaw.

(Turn to page 61)

"No, of course not," Dr. Bayless replies. "Where on earth did you get an idea like that? I was just going to have my assistant give you a crowbar so we could start prying the lid off Anankha's burial vault."

"I'm confused, Dad," Lisa says as you sigh in relief. "Why did you say that *you* were the only one who was going to get rich from all of this?"

"Oh, I didn't say that," her father explains, handing you a crowbar. "I said that I was the only one who was going to get anything out of it. I'll publish papers in the scholarly journals, and be invited to speak at conferences all over the world to discuss our findings here."

"But what about the treasure?" you ask. "Don't we get to keep what we find?" You begin to pry at the lid of the vault, along with Dr. Bayless and the others.

"I'm afraid not," Dr. Bayless grunts. "Whatever treasures we find belong to the Egyptian government. We aren't allowed to keep anything."

"Then what are we doing here?" Lisa asks.

Dr. Bayless pauses to wipe his forehead with a handkerchief. "It's my job, Lisa. I'm an archaeologist. Think of the knowledge to be gained from exploring the tomb of Anankha."

"I'd rather think of the treasure," Lisa says glumly.

"Or the curse of Anankha," you add, even more glumly. You haven't forgotten the curse: *Painful and violent death will be the reward of whoever enters this chamber and disturbs the slumber of Anankha.*

Then, underscoring your thoughts, the slab of rock covering the burial vault begins to groan in protest as it slides ever so slowly away from the vault.

"It's coming," Dr. Bayless grunts as he and the workmen lean against their pries and levers.

Then the slab is away, revealing the contents of the stone vault. You help Dr. Bayless, Lisa, and the workmen gently lower the heavy slab to the floor.

Lisa is the first to inspect the vault. As everyone else is straightening, she shines her light into the open grave, gasps, and stares at the contents with unbelieving eyes.

You rise. Gripping the side of the vault for support, you lean over the exposed top, staring inside.

Less than two feet away, the Egyptian cobra watches you, its lidless, red eyes gleaming like evil beacons. Coiled and ready to strike at the first sign of movement, the snake is poised to inflict its deadly bite, and thus to fulfill the curse of Anankha. You freeze in unbelieving horror, wanting to run, to shout, or to do anything besides stand there staring helplessly at the cobra before you.

(Turn to page 64)

"Let me go, Terry!" you grunt.

"Sure." Terry releases you. "You're not my type, anyway." Terry is taller and heavier than you. He looks even larger in the thick, bulky sweater he's wearing.

"Where's Lisa?" you ask casually, trying to hide your surprise at finding Terry in the middle of the woods.

"Here I am," a voice replies from behind you. You turn to find Lisa stepping from behind the large boulder.

Lisa and Terry are your best friends. They came along with your family on your vacation to the mountains this summer.

You eye them suspiciously. "I thought you said last night that you didn't want to go hiking this morning."

Lisa looks at Terry and smiles. "We changed our minds. The air is so fresh and clean, and everything is so pretty early in the morning."

"Yeah," Terry adds, "and besides, your dad wanted the car washed this morning. And you and Mitchie were gone."

For the first time you notice that Mitchie isn't present. When Terry appeared from out of nowhere, you naturally assumed that Mitchie was with him.

"Where's Mitchie?" you ask.

Terry shrugs his shoulders. "We thought he was with you."

"Uh-uh." You explain how you and Mitchie became separated. "I think he's lost," you say finally.

"I don't know about Mitchie, but *we're* lost," Lisa says.

"No, we're not," Terry argues.

Lisa places her hands on her hips. "Okay, smarty. If you know so much, where are we right now?"

Terry walks over and places a hand on the large boulder. "See this rock?"

You and Lisa nod without smiling.

Grizzly!

"Get ready," Lisa whispers, *"Terry's going to s[ay something] stupid."*

"I heard that," Terry says, "but you can't ins[ult me. I've] been insulted by experts!" Terry pats the rock. "Here is where we are. Right here, standing next to this big rock."

"We *know* that," Lisa says patiently in the same tone of voice she uses when she's talking to Mitchie or other dumb animals. "But if we're *here*, which way is it to the cabin?"

"Sorry," Terry replies. "Only one question to a customer."

"I think I can find our way back," you say, "but first we've got to find Mitchie."

"Why?" Terry asks.

"You know, Terry," Lisa says, "if you were shorter, greener, and smarter, you could get a job as a cabbage."

Terry laughs. "Yeah, but they'd have to pay me a good *celery.*"

You and Lisa glance at each other and groan.

Suddenly, you hear a voice calling as if from far away.

"It's Mitchie!" Lisa says.

"What's he saying?" Terry asks.

"If you'll be quiet, you might find out," Lisa hisses.

"Mitchie," you call loudly, ignoring Terry and Lisa's arguing. "Can you hear me? Where are you?"

"I'm over here," Mitchie's voice replies, closer this time. He says something else, but you can't quite make out his words.

"I think he said he's in trouble," Lisa says.

Then you're running, pounding through dark green thickets of mountain laurel and rhododendrons. Behind you, Terry and Lisa are making as much noise as a marching band. Despite yourself, you wonder if grizzlies or mountain lions are attracted to noises in the deep forest.

Dad says that sometimes at night a grizzly will come right up to your campfire out of curiosity. If you're sleeping when it comes, you might not even know that it's been there until the next morning, when you wake up to find a grizzly's footprints on the ground around your sleeping bag. But if you're *not* sleeping when it comes, or if the grizzly happens to be particularly hungry—well, it's better not to think about things like that.

"Hey," Mitchie calls out, "I'm over here!"

You stop suddenly, glancing to your right. Mitchie is sitting on the edge of a large rock, waving.

"Mitchie, are you all right?" Lisa cries. Mitchie doesn't seem to understand what she's said.

"I can't hear you," Mitchie shouts. And that's bad news, because Mitchie isn't alone. Towering above and behind him, and roaring like a grizzly bear but twice as large, is an enormous

(Turn to page 66)

Your first stunned reaction is that Terry has gone crazy. But as you watch, at the very last second, he slows his hand, spreads his fingers, and swats at the mosquito that is biting Lisa's cheek.

"Missed!" Terry says disgustedly.

"No, you didn't," Lisa replies, rubbing her jaw.

Terry frowns. "Next time, you can kill your own mosquitos."

Forty-five minutes later, the four of you are settled down for the night in your tents. You, Lisa, and Terry are using small pup tents; Uncle Ned has disappeared inside a large canvas tent equipped with mosquito netting.

"Lisa, are you awake?" you call out softly.

"Yes," she whispers. Her tent is only a few yards from yours.

"How about you, Terry?" you ask, but there's no answer.

"He's asleep," Lisa whispers. "I heard him snoring a few minutes ago."

You turn your head in the direction of Terry's tent, and that's when you feel it: *there's something on your neck.* And it's not a mosquito, either. It's about sixteen inches long, it's round—and worst of all, it's moving. You lie back in your sleeping bag, hardly daring to breathe.

The first thought that enters your mind is: *it's a coral snake! There's a coral snake in my sleeping bag!*

(Turn to page 68)

You feel a tapping on your shoulder. You turn to find Lisa watching you with a curious expression on her face. Seeing her jars you back to reality.

There's no great white shark.

It was all a daydream. A terrible, nightmarish daydream. Still, it's over. You don't know whether to feel relieved or angry for scaring yourself so badly.

Lisa gestures and points toward shore. You nod in agreement. You're beginning to believe that the ocean *is* a spooky place, after all.

As you turn to leave, a movement from out of the darkness at the entrance to the cave catches your eye. The grayish shape lunges at you, and before you can move it has fastened itself to you with hundreds of disc-shaped suckers.

It's a giant octopus, wrapping its deadly tentacles about you!

(Turn to page 83)

The snake, made of gold and inlaid with colored glass and precious stones, adorns the headdress of Anankha's funeral mask. The mask, bearing the likeness of Anankha, has been fitted onto his mummified remains.

"It's so beautiful!" Lisa exclaims.

"Yes, it is," her father replies. "Too bad he couldn't have taken it with him on his journey to the Realm of the Dead." Lisa glances sharply at him, but he goes right on.

"The ancient Egyptians believed that when you died your spirit, or soul, went on a long, dangerous journey to the Realm of the Dead. Thus, they usually left food, clothing, jewelry, weapons, tools, and even furniture in their tombs with the mummy. Sometimes they buried wives or servants with the departed, to guide and protect the soul on its journey."

"Too bad they couldn't just send off for AAA Tour Guides," you mumble, staring at the gold death mask.

Lisa frowns at you. "Why did they prepare mummies, anyway?" she asks her father.

Dr. Bayless adjusts his glasses. "They believed that the soul would be happier if the body were preserved. So they figured out a way to embalm the body, dry it out, and wrap it so that it would keep for centuries."

A shudder of sudden fear passes through you like wind whispering through the trees. You can't believe that you're standing here in a tomb, twenty feet underground, calmly discussing burial procedures used by the ancient Egyptians. You just know that, when the funeral mask is lifted away from the remains beneath it, the mummy is going to sit up, an empty eye socket peering at you through the rotted remains of its linen shroud.

And then, as you gaze blankly at the undead pharaoh,

unable to move from where you stand, a bony hand covered by leathery skin snakes out of the darkness and clamps down on your collarbone.

(Turn to page 69)

waterfall.

"Mitchie, be careful!" Lisa shouts. "There's a waterfall behind you!"

Mitchie shakes his head. "I can't hear you. There's a water-fall behind me!"

When the three of you reach Mitchie, you're relieved to find that he's safe and unharmed. "I'm hungry," Mitchie says.

"Me, too," Lisa chimes in. "Let's go back and have some breakfast."

"Uh-oh," Terry says. "It looks like *we're* going to be break-fast."

Lisa begins to speak, but stops when she sees the sick expression on Terry's face. Slowly, her gaze slides to her left, away from Terry.

Sixty yards away, a dark shape emerges from behind a thicket of mountain laurels.

"It's a bear!" Mitchie shouts.

"Hush, Mitchie," you whisper. "If we keep quiet, maybe it won't see us."

The bear—a large adult male grizzly—has seen you, though. It pauses to sniff the air, and then rises to full height on two legs. It paws the air angrily.

The silvery gray grizzly stands nine feet tall.

"What'll we do?" Lisa asks helplessly.

"I don't know what *you're* worried about, Lisa," Terry hisses. "It's probably a man-eater. *I'm* the one who should be worried!"

Meanwhile, you're trying to control the rising tide of panic within you. There has to be a way out of this, but you'll never find it if you give in to your fear.

The grizzly drops to all fours. Without a moment's hesitation, it begins to gallop toward you. Even from sixty yards away, you can hear the *huff!—huff!—huff!—*of its breathing as it runs.

"Run!" Lisa shouts.

But there's no time to run, and nowhere to go. In less than six seconds either you or one of your friends is going to fall victim to the grizzly's attack.

"No!" you shout. "Don't run! We'd never make it! Quick, everybody up a tree!"

You race for the nearest tree and swing up into its lower limbs. On either side of you, Terry and Lisa are scurrying up their trees like human elevators.

Below you, Mitchie is crying loudly. "Help me, I can't reach the limb," he pleads.

And forty yards away, the big grizzly is galloping toward Mitchie with a speed that is surprising for an animal weighing more than half a ton.

(Turn to page 72)

The second thought that enters your mind is: *It's only the medallion and chain I'm wearing around my neck. I should have taken it off before I climbed into my sleeping bag.*

You reach up and unzip the sleeping bag, intending to sit up and take off the medallion so you can store it in a safe place. Before you can do so, however, an unearthly roar pierces the night air, followed by a heavy weight descending onto your tent, collapsing it.

"Terry, stop it!" you shout, raising your hands to protect your head as whoever or whatever is out there begins to pound on the collapsed tent. But there's no answer—nothing except harsh growls and an occasional scream of rage as the pounding and pushing continue.

"C'mon, Terry, cut it out! This isn't funny any more!" you yell angrily. Terry doesn't stop, though. Inside the pup tent, you curl up into a ball to protect yourself, hoping that Terry will grow tired of his little game.

Finally, you manage to reach out and grab an edge of the tent. You jerk it away, ready to bawl Terry out for his late-night prank.

But it isn't Terry.

The hideous face snarling into yours from inches away is like nothing you've ever seen. And it certainly isn't human.

(Turn to page 75)

"I'm back," Terry says.

"Everything come out all right?" Lisa asks sarcastically.

"Yeah, but you better watch where you step when we're leaving." Then, eyeing the mummy and its death mask, Terry releases you and steps to the edge of the vault. "Hey, neat! Dad should be here to see this: a real live mummy!"

"Send him a postcard," Lisa says drily. "One of those that says 'Wish you were here.' "

Dr. Bayless reaches down and lifts the funeral mask away from the mummy.

For an insane moment you think you see the mummy move slightly. A twitch of its hand, perhaps, or maybe a slight turning of its head in your direction. But no one else seems to have noticed anything, so you manage to convince yourself that it didn't happen. You were just seeing things.

At least, you hope you were.

The mummy is wrapped in narrow strips of cloth that are yellow with age and stained in places.

Dr. Bayless draws a pair of surgical scissors from his pocket, then glances up at you, Terry, and Lisa. "I'm going to cut away the wrappings, but you don't have to stay if you don't want to."

"I wouldn't miss it for the world," Terry says.

You and Lisa exchange glances, then nod weakly.

"We'll stay," Lisa says in a voice barely above a whisper.

The task takes longer than you thought it would. Dr. Bayless is as careful and sure-handed as a surgeon, and unbinding Anankha proceeds at a snail's pace for nearly two hours. Finally, Dr. Bayless steps away from his work.

You, Terry, and Lisa stare at the mummy.

"Doesn't look so hot, does he?" Terry asks. "I think he ought to see a doctor or something."

"He already saw a doctor," you reply. "That's why he's here."

"Let's see how *you* look after five thousand years, Terry," Lisa snorts.

"I bet I'll look better than *that*," Terry says, wrinkling his nose. "He reminds me of our geography teacher, Mr. Hodgkins."

"Actually," Dr. Bayless says, "Anankha was quite a handsome young man."

"How do you know that?" you ask, eyeing the mummy with disgust.

"This shows us what he looked like," Dr. Bayless replies, holding up the funeral mask. "It's probably an almost perfect likeness."

"I still think he looks like Mr. Hodgkins," Terry says.

"I think he's cute," Lisa says, giggling.

"And I think it's about time for us to stop for lunch," Dr. Bayless says, checking his watch.

You're outside, eating your lunch and leaning back against a small hill, trying to take advantage of a thin sliver of shadow. The midday heat is incredible; it must be at least 120° in the shade!

Terry eyes the meat on his plate suspiciously, turning it over with his fork. "What is this stuff, anyway? Somebody better check to see if one of the camels is missing!"

"Aw, quit complaining, Terry," you say irritably.

"Me? Complain? I don't know what you're talking about," Terry replies. "Just because this meat looks like the mummy—"

Terry halts in midsentence, staring at the top of the hill two feet above your head. You turn to see what he's looking at.

"It's a scorpion," Terry says dumbly.

"Where?" Lisa asks, swiveling her head upward.

As if in reply to her question, the scorpion slips off the edge of the hill and drops down like a falling leaf. It lands feet-first on your shoulder with the deadly stinger at the end of its tail poised like the spear of a javelin thrower.

(Turn to page 76)

You reach down and lift Mitchie into the lower branches of the slender tree you're in. The two of you scamper up the tree like a couple of squirrels.

When you reach a point twelve feet above the ground, you look down to find the enraged grizzly reaching for you. Its huge claws are a scant six inches away from your foot.

"C'mon, Mitchie, climb higher!" you urge as the bear roars deafeningly.

"It's okay, I'm safe up here," Mitchie replies from above you.

"Well, I'm not! Besides, you're standing on my hand."

As Mitchie climbs, he glances down at the bear and asks, "Do you think he'll come after us?"

"No, grizzlies don't climb trees very well. They're too big."

"That's good. I don't think all of us would fit up here."

You and Mitchie continue to climb, higher and higher. But as you reach the upper branches, the tree begins to sway back and forth in a broad arc.

"He's trying to shake us out of the tree!" Mitchie shouts.

Below, the grizzly is standing erect on two feet with its forepaws gripping the tree tightly. The bear leans forward, then backward, and then forward again, alternately pushing and pulling the slender tree.

Huddled together in the treetop, you and Mitchie are whipped from side to side like a pair of windshield wipers. Over the pounding of your heart you can hear Lisa screaming from somewhere nearby and the angry grizzly snarling below you.

"Hang on, Mitchie!" you shout. "Don't let go!"

"But what if the tree breaks in two?" Mitchie wails.

Suddenly, without wanting to do so, you recall the old nursery rhyme:

When the bough breaks, the cradle will fall
And down will come baby, cradle and all.

You'd rather not think about that, though. Because if the bough breaks, there's an angry, 1000-pound grizzly bear waiting down below to break your fall—and maybe break your neck as well.

"We've got to get out of here!" you shout.

"Yes, but how?" Mitchie asks.

For the first time in a long while, you hear Terry's voice. He's in a nearby tree, hanging on for dear life.

"Grab hold of my tree next time you swing this way. It's bigger than yours. He won't be able to shake you down from this one!"

Suddenly, you hear a cracking sound a few feet below you as the treetop snaps violently back and forth.

The tree is beginning to splinter!

Soon, you realize, the entire upper section is going to break off. You have to act now, before your weight and the bear's shaking sends the treetop crashing to the ground!

Without pausing to think, you time the tree's swaying, and as you swing toward Terry's tree you release your grip and leap.

Thirty feet below you, the grizzly watches hopefully as you hurtle through space like a flying squirrel.

(Turn to page 80)

Somewhere in the darkness, you hear Lisa screaming insanely. You can't hear what she's saying, but it doesn't matter. All that matters is the ghastly face with long, yellowed fangs dipping toward your unprotected throat.

It's the Thing in the Swamp.

And now that you've seen it, you're going to die. It can't afford to let you live. For its own safety, you have to die.

(Turn to page 81)

"Don't move," Terry says. As Lisa watches, horrified, Terry reaches over and gently flicks the scorpion off your shoulder.

It lands in Lisa's lap.

She leaps to her feet with a shriek. "Terry, you lamebrain, are you trying to kill us?"

Terry laughs. "No sweat, Lisa. It's dead. It was dead when it fell. Probably, it got caught out in the sun, had heatstroke, and zapped itself with its stinger. Scorpions do that, you know."

He sits back, smiling smugly, with his hands behind his head.

"This one didn't," Lisa says, pointing at the scorpion, which is skittering along the rubble at the base of the hill, heading for Terry.

"The scorpion's revenge," you mutter as the three of you leap to your feet and dance away.

The rest of the afternoon is spent in feverish activity, with Dr. Bayless telling everyone how to catalog the tomb's contents. Then it's time for a sponge bath to wash away the day's collected dirt and grime, a quick supper, and then to bed in order to get an early start tomorrow.

You lie in your small tent, waiting. The day's incredible heat is gone now; there's even a slight chill in the air. Or is it just tiny prickles of fear that are causing you to shiver as you lie on your cot, waiting?

Waiting for Terry.

You know he's coming. You know, too, that he'll persuade you to do precisely what you'd rather not do than anything else in the world: he's going to talk you into going back into the tomb of Anankha tonight. By yourselves, of course.

And you know that, if you listen to Terry and re-enter the tomb, you'll never come out alive.

Five minutes later, Terry's head pops into the opening in your tent. "C'mon, get dressed. Let's go," he whispers.

Arguing with Terry is useless; you may as well be arguing with a rock. Terry won't take no for an answer. He never does.

"Hey, you're already dressed," Terry says as you climb out of bed and slip your shoes on. "I knew I could count on you!"

"Is Lisa coming with us?"

"Uh-uh," Terry replies, shaking his head. "She's already asleep."

"My flashlight isn't working," you say, searching for an excuse not to go with Terry.

He hands you a flashlight. "This one is. Lisa and I fixed yours earlier so it wouldn't work, but this one is brand new. I borrowed it from Dr. Bayless after supper tonight."

"I don't know what I'd do without friends like you and Lisa," you grumble, rising and stepping outside into the Egyptian night.

"Hey, what are friends for?" Terry whispers.

"I've wondered that myself," you reply, dreading the ordeal in store for you.

The Egyptian worker guarding the entrance to the tomb smiles broadly as you approach. Terry smiles and returns the greeting. As the two of you enter the dark stairway leading down into the tomb's depths, the workman whispers, "Be careful." The way he pronounces it sounds like *Bee carefool.*

We're fools, all right, you think as Terry leads you along the narrow stairway.

Down, down, down you go, feeling your way cautiously in the darkness. The stairway seems to be longer and steeper than it was earlier, the darkness deeper despite the glow of your two flashlights.

A feeling of dread clings to you like wet clothing. You feel as if some kind of powerful and evil force is drawing you ever closer to itself.

"Terry, I don't like this. Let's get out of here," you whisper as you reach the foot of the stairs.

"Aw, c'mon, be a sport," Terry says. The two of you turn the corner and walk slowly toward the burial chamber fifty feet ahead.

Halfway down the long corridor you pause. "Terry, wait a minute. I'm scared. I don't think we should be in here like this. There's something evil about this place."

Terry pauses, turns, and directs his flashlight beam at your face. "Hey, you really are scared, aren't you?"

You nod, feeling as if your arms and legs weigh a ton apiece.

Terry stares at you, thinking. "Tell you what," he says finally. "I'll go in there, and you can wait for me here."

"Okay," you say weakly.

Terry turns back to the passageway. "I won't be long." Beyond him, faintly outlined against the utter darkness on either side of it, the doorway to the burial chamber yawns open like the gaping mouth of a monster from your nightmares.

Suddenly, a booming sound coming from somewhere behind you echoes through the lonely corridor.

"What was that?" Fear makes your voice a high-pitched squeak.

"I don't know," Terry says. His voice is less confident than before.

"I think we ought to get out of here—now!" you gasp.

"Maybe you're right," Terry says. He shines his light toward the room at the end of the passageway. "But I really wanted to . . ."

"Terry, what is it? What's the matter?" you ask in a trembling voice.

He steps aside, trying to point, but his hands fall limply to his sides. His face is frozen, bloodless. His mouth is working, trying to form words, but nothing comes out.

Slowly, you shift your flashlight's beam from Terry to the doorway to the burial chamber—and almost drop the flashlight as weakness washes over you like a tidal wave.

There, in the doorway with arms outstretched to receive you, stands the mummified remains of Anankha. Beside him, dressed in a faded, rotting linen gown, is the grinning skeleton of his young bride.

(Turn to page 87)

You soar through the air with arms outstretched, reaching for the tree. It slams into you with a force that almost takes your breath away. You hardly notice the pain, though, as you wrap your arms around the tree and scramble for a foothold in the branches.

Ten feet below you, Terry is standing on a large limb.

You glance at your little brother in the other tree. "C'mon, Mitchie, jump! I'll catch you!"

"I can't!" Mitchie wails.

"You've got to," you shout. "The tree is going to break off below you. I'll catch you when you jump!"

Mitchie is hanging onto the tree with both arms, staring at you uncertainly through eyes filled with tears.

"Well . . . okay, if you promise to catch me."

You're on the verge of panic as you hear another loud, cracking sound. "Come on, it's got to be *now*, Mitchie!" You extend an arm toward him, trying to look confident.

The tree sways toward you. Mitchie takes a final, deep breath and then leaps, arms flailing wildly.

For a moment, he seems to be suspended in air as the tree-top snaps and falls away below him.

You reach for Mitchie with your fingers spread to grasp any part of him you can reach. Even as you do so, however, your heart sinks. You can tell that he's not going to make it.

When the treetop broke, it reduced the distance of Mitchie's leap.

You can only watch helplessly, screaming his name as Mitchie begins to fall away toward the grizzly bear waiting below.

(Turn to page 92)

You struggle against your attacker, but it's no use. You might as well be trying to stop the wind from blowing.

The monster slowly forces you onto your back. Against your will, you find your gaze being drawn to the beast's face. There, barely six inches away, you find huge, gaping jaws filled with long, razor-sharp teeth, and deep-set eyes glaring at you with undisguised hatred.

And on one of the monster's plastic cheeks is a tag that reads, *$1.89.*

"Pretty good mask, huh?" Terry says, chuckling. "I got it at the Mall."

"So I noticed," you grunt as Lisa explodes in uncontrolled laughter.

"C'mon, admit it," Terry says. "You were scared, weren't you?"

"I'll admit I was scared if you'll get off me."

"Okay." Terry climbs to his feet and moves over by Lisa. "Well?" he says.

"All right, I was scared—a little. I was afraid you'd crush me, you big tub of lard!"

"Hey, we were only joking, weren't we, Lisa?" Terry says. But Lisa doesn't answer. She can't. All she can do is stare in speechless terror at the enormous, dark shape that is emerging silently from the misty shoreline of the lake behind her.

"Uncle Ned, help! It's the Thing in the Swamp!" Terry shouts, backing away slowly from the Thing in the water.

At first, you're tempted to believe that the dark shape climbing out of the water *is* Uncle Ned; but no, the great beast's arms are outstretched to the sides, and in the center of its forehead is a single eye that casts a powerful beam like a searchlight.

"It *is* the Thing in the Swamp!" you gasp, stumbling back-ward. As you turn to run, your foot catches on a root and down you go.

"Wait!" you call out as Lisa and Terry flee into the night in blind terror. But before you can rise, the Thing rushes toward you, reaches down with one hand, and jerks you to your feet in one swift motion. You turn to find the teeth

(Turn to page 89)

Fortunately, it's a *baby* giant octopus. Its tentacles are only four inches long.

Still, it *is* an octopus, and as far as you're concerned they're the most disgusting animals you can think of. Except for your little brother Mitchie, that is.

You pry the little animal loose from your arm. It squirts a small cloud of inky fluid in your direction, then scurries back to the safety of the cave.

It's time to get back to shore, all right.

You and Lisa swim away from the underwater cave, away from the drop-off and the whale shark. Gradually, the water changes color from sapphire blue to blue-green, and finally to a clear emerald green as you draw closer and closer to shore.

Then you and Lisa are standing in waist-deep water, admiring the view. Fifty yards ahead, waves lap gently at the white beach.

Beyond the beach, tall palm trees stand guard like sentries in front of a thick green jungle.

"Beautiful, isn't it?" you say, meaning the primitive setting. It's as if you and Lisa have somehow stumbled into the Garden of Eden, a place of perfect beauty. You feel as if the two of you are the only people left on earth to share the unspoiled beauty of your surroundings.

Lisa nods in agreement. "And there aren't any sharks in there."

"There aren't any sharks *here*, either," you reply. "The water is too shallow. And besides—"

Suddenly, a movement attracts your attention. You turn to find a large shape hurtling toward you in the water. Dimly, you hear Lisa screaming as if from far away. You open your mouth in surprise, but before you can utter a sound, the dark

shape crashes into you, sending you tumbling backward under-water.

Stunned, you hardly feel it when the jaws of a great white shark clamp down around your middle.

I must be dreaming! you think frantically. But then, as pain begins to spread through your midsection, you glance down. Blood—your blood—is swirling in the water around you.

It's no dream. And one glance at the fearsome set of razor-sharp, inch-long triangular teeth convinces you that they belong to a great white shark.

(Turn to page 97)

The two figures—Anankha and his bride—are moving slowly toward you. Anankha walks with a limp, dragging his right leg along in a *sssssssss*—step—*sssssssss*—step movement.

"I—I must be dreaming!" Terry says. He pinches himself on the arm, then yelps with pain. "Ow! I'm not dreaming."

You lean over and pinch Terry on the arm. His shriek of pain tells you that you're not dreaming, either.

The ghostly figures are ten feet away. Then eight feet. Then five. Reaching for you, from beyond time and the grave.

"I don't know about you," Terry mutters weakly, "but *I'm* gettin' outa here!"

Somehow, you find strength in your rubbery legs to run after Terry.

The two of you turn the corner in the passageway, then dash up the steep stairway . . . only to find the entrance blocked by the same large stone that concealed the entrance from outsiders for five thousand years!

You hear the sound of someone screaming in the dark tunnel, and you're only vaguely aware that it is you who is screaming. Dimly, you realize that the booming sound you heard earlier must have been the stone rolling back into place against the entrance.

But that couldn't be, you realize, unless . . .

Unless Anankha caused it to happen.

And that couldn't be, either, unless . . .

Unless Anankha isn't dead.

He's been waiting for you. For five thousand years, he's been waiting for someone like you to take his place.

You and Terry push at the rock, pound on it, and scream for help, but to no avail. No one can hear you. The stone is wedged so snugly against the entrance that not even air can enter the passageway.

You're trapped, with no way out of the tomb.

And somewhere below you in the darkness, the mummy and his bride begin to climb the steep stairway, reaching with arms outstretched to embrace you in a grisly dance of death.

(Turn to page 93)

of Uncle Ned gleaming in a broad grin. A miner's light is attached to a band around his forehead. Uncle Ned laughs loudly.

"Terry, Lisa, come back! Everything is all right!" he calls. They return to the campfire with embarrassed grins on their faces.

"I knew it was Uncle Ned all the time," Terry says sheepishly.

"Sure you did," Lisa replies sarcastically. "That's why you were gone like a shot as soon as you saw him."

"Aw, I was just going along with the gag," Terry says unconvincingly.

"Yeah, and I'm the Tooth Fairy," you reply.

Lisa turns to Terry's uncle. "What were you doing out there, Uncle Ned? Trying to scare us?"

Uncle Ned throws back his head and laughs heartily. "It looks like you three were doing a pretty good job of scaring yourselves without my help."

He pauses. "No, actually I was out doing a bit of frog gigging." He holds up four fat frogs he has caught. "We'll have froglegs for supper tomorrow night. But you three were making so much noise that I couldn't concentrate on my work."

"We thought you were the Thing in the Swamp," Lisa blurts out. "I-I mean, we saw the light, and . . ."

"Aw, that's just an old story. There ain't no Thing in the Swamp," Terry says.

"You didn't think so five minutes ago," Lisa sputters angrily.

"Don't dismiss it so easily, Terry," Uncle Ned says. "Remember, I saw the footprints. And Lisa was closer to the truth than she thought she was. The Indian legends sometimes mentioned a loud roaring and a bright light accompanying the creature."

"You mean like *that* loud noise and bright light?" Terry asks, pointing behind Uncle Ned.

Four pairs of eyes turn toward the lake, where a low, growl-

ing noise is quickly growing into an unearthly roar. A light, growing brighter with every passing second, means only one thing: whatever is out there in the darkness is heading directly toward you, and at an incredible rate of speed.

"It's the Thing," Uncle Ned shouts. "Run, kids! Run for your lives! *It's coming!*"

Seized by sudden panic, you turn and sprint away blindly into the night. Forgotten are your friends Terry and Lisa. All that matters is putting as much distance as possible between you and the Thing in the Swamp.

(Turn to page 95)

"Gotcha!" Terry says, grasping Mitchie by the back of his gray sweatshirt. Terry hauls Mitchie into the tree, where he latches onto the trunk and sobs loudly.

"That was close," you mutter, weak with relief.

Twenty minutes later, having grown tired of trying to shake you out of the larger tree, the grizzly leaves. Forty-five minutes after that, the four of you decide that maybe it's safe for you to climb down and go home.

Slowly, cautiously, you climb down from your trees. When all of you are on solid ground again, you, Terry, and Lisa find yourselves laughing with relief.

"I don't know what you're laughing about," Mitchie says unhappily. "I was scared." You laugh even harder.

You laugh so hard, in fact, that none of you hears the animal padding softly toward you in the underbrush.

"That's just like you, Mitchie," Terry begins.

He never finishes his sentence.

Without warning, a pair of huge paws clamps down tightly on Terry's shoulders.

(Turn to page 94)

Terry, who by now is whimpering and crying like a baby, flings his flashlight down the stairway. It bounces off Anankha and clatters to the floor, its beam extinguished.

"That was smart," you say, scowling at Terry. Below, the mummy is advancing onto the eighth step. His bride is a step below him, grinning from ear to ear. Only she has no ears.

"Well, we've got to do something," Terry babbles. "What else is there to do? Invite them to sit down and play a few hands of gin rummy?"

"But we needed the light," you reply weakly as the mummy reaches the fifteenth step.

"Why? So we can watch them tearing us apart?"

Anankha is at the twentieth step, only eight steps below you. Terry screams for help—but even if someone outside hears him, they'll never be able to move the stone away from the entrance in time to rescue you.

The mummy pauses on the twenty-fourth step. When it speaks, its breath carries an odor of rotten eggs.

"*You . . . should have . . . heeded . . . the . . . warning. Now . . . you must . . . die . . . a violent and . . . painful . . . death . . . death . . . death . . .*"

(Turn to page 98)

Terry leaps in fright, and spins to push away your German shepherd Ralph, who is busily trying to lick Terry's face.

Behind Ralph, your father and a forest ranger are approaching.

"Dad, you'll never believe what's happened to us!" you shout in relief as Mitchie runs to him and hugs him tightly.

"And you'll never believe what's going to happen to you when we get back to the cabin, either," Dad says sternly. Then his features soften. "Are you all right?"

"Sure," Terry replies casually. "There was a bear, and—"

"We know," the ranger says. "We found it a few minutes ago. It's an old grizzly that we've been looking for. We shot it with a tranquilizer dart and caged it."

"Why did you do that?" Mitchie asks.

"Oh, it's an old bear; it has taken to raiding hen houses lately. We want to relocate it somewhere farther away from humans."

"Anybody hungry?" Dad asks. Four voices answer *Yes!* "Great. Your mother has breakfast ready." He turns and walks away.

"And after breakfast," Dad continues, "the four of you are going on another hike. This time—"

He raises a hand to silence four groans of protest. "This time, though, you can hike down to the stream to get some water to wash the car with!"

The End

"Wait! Hold it, I was just kidding," Uncle Ned shouts as the three of you rush headlong into the night and away from the lake. You don't believe him, though, not until you hear him roaring with laughter.

He's *laughing*?

You, Terry, and Lisa stop and turn around slowly, then look at each other in amazement.

Uncle Ned is walking toward the lake. He pauses, hands on hips, waiting. His body is bathed in the strange, bright light.

"What's he doing?" Terry asks. He has to talk loudly to be heard over the deafening roar.

Then a strange thing happens. The roar quiets down to a soft murmur, then stops entirely. The light blinks out. Uncle Ned's voice breaks the sudden stillness of the night.

"That you, Roy?"

"Yeah," another voice replies. "Who else were you expecting at this time of night, Santa Claus?"

Uncle Ned turns to face you. "It's okay, kids. Sorry I played such a trick on you, but I couldn't resist it. I guess I'm a kid at heart myself."

The man called Roy steps out of the airboat he arrived in and joins Uncle Ned.

"This is Roy McKinnon," Uncle Ned says. "Roy's a ranger for the park service. He came out to check on us."

"You—you mean you *knew* he was coming?" Lisa asks.

"Sure." Uncle Ned beams. "Roy always comes out to check on me when I stay overnight in the swamp. Maybe tomorrow he'll come back and take you for a ride in his airboat."

"Glad to," Roy says as you, Lisa, and Terry stare at the two men.

"What's the matter?" Roy asks. "You three look like you've seen a ghost."

"Don't mention that word," Lisa groans.

"Hey, c'mon," Terry says, grinning, "you know there's no such things as ghosts or monsters."

And at that very moment, somewhere deep in the swamp but not so very far away, a huge beast larger and stronger than a bear prowls the night, searching for its next victim. It pauses, sniffs the air, then begins walking quietly toward the campsite where you and your friends are spending the night.

The End

Lisa is still screaming when your head bobs above the surface. Only she's not screaming at you or the shark.

"Terry, you idiot, you almost scared us to death!"

Terry Willis is standing in the waist-deep water laughing like crazy. He's wearing a mask and snorkel, and holding up an enormous set of shark jaws for you to see. "Neat, huh?" he manages to say between waves of laughter. "They belonged to a great white shark. I knew you'd want to see them up close."

Terry glances at your stomach and sees the line of shallow scratches zigzagging across it. "Sorry 'bout that—but you know how sharks are when they smell blood in the water."

"Yeah," you agree, wading toward Terry, "and when I catch you, you'll think *you* were in a fight with a great white shark!"

Then the three of you are off, laughing and splashing your way through the shallow waters in search of other adventures. And in the ocean, excitement, adventure, and danger are seldom more than a step or two away.

The End

. . . death of me—I don't know where your mind is," says Mr. Hodgkins, your geography teacher.

He's standing over you, arms folded across his chest, staring down at you. The expression on his face is anything but pleasant.

"I don't know what we're going to do about you," Mr. Hodgkins continues. "Here we are studying about Egypt, and your mind is somewhere else a million miles away."

"I'm sorry, I must have been daydreaming," you say. "It won't happen again."

Mr. Hodgkins eyes you suspiciously. "Well, see that it doesn't." He returns to his desk at the front of the room.

You try to return to your lessons, but two questions keep turning over and over in your mind.

Where is Terry? (He was in his seat at the beginning of the period.)

And where did the flashlight come from that you have in your hand?

The End

About the Author

Dr. William E. Warren is an educator with nineteen years of teaching experience at all levels ranging from elementary through university. He has written several books of nonfiction as well as textbooks and magazine articles. His first book of fiction for young people, *The Graveyard and Other Not-So-Scary Stories*, published by Prentice-Hall, reflects his love of humor and of scary tales. Dr. Warren has had a great deal of experience in working with children; he has coached various sports, has been an athletic director and camp counselor, and he now teaches world history. Besides reading, Dr. Warren's interests include folk singing, playing the guitar, jogging, and writing. He and his wife Eleanor live in Vidalia, Georgia.

About the Artist

Edward Frascino was born in the Bronx and grew up in Yonkers, New York. His fascination with comic strips and movies as a child led him to study art at Parsons School of Design. His cartoons appear regularly in *The New Yorker, The New York Times,* and *Saturday Review,* and they have recently been collected in one volume, *Avocado Is Not Your Color.* Mr. Frascino is the author of *Eddie Spaghetti,* a popular children's novel, and the illustrator of *Oh, Brother!,* a joke collection published by Prentice-Hall, and of the first book by William E. Warren, *The Graveyard and Other Not-So-Scary Stories.* He lives in Brooklyn, New York.

3